❧ DITTO

FUNK & WAGNALLS · NEW YORK

..DITTO

BY BARBARA CLAYTON

Illustrated by Sandra Willcox

1

U. S. 1442357

For Grandma and Grandpa Pluff

Other books by the same author

☙ Contents

DITTO

1 ❧ Feet First

A piercing whistle echoed across the meadow. Bugle barked, and Diane ran to the window of the pottery. Darryl and Spider Appleton and Bruce Eaton were chasing one another through the apple orchard. Then the three members of the Whale's Creek Ghosts disappeared over the brow of the meadow.

As she dusted the soft-hued pottery mugs, Diane stared wistfully after the boys. For the last hour, car after car had jounced down the old rutted road which wound through the apple orchard and led to the bathing beach on the shore. On the Fourth of July, everyone in Whale's Neck turned out for the annual Lobster Picnic at Whale's Creek.

"Whale's Creek, Maine," Grandfather Jordan had explained to Diane when she first arrived from Missouri, "is a suburb of Whale's Neck." He'd added, chuckling, "All three houses."

Grandfather's pottery sat on the edge of the road, and his house—a short distance from the pottery—was the middle one of the three houses. The Appleton Farm, where Darryl and Spider lived, was beyond the apple orchard, and Bruce Eaton lived on the other side of the creek. Diane had met the boys soon after she'd flown from St. Louis to visit Grandfather Jordan for the summer. It wasn't exactly a visit, though, and Diane hoped very much it wouldn't be for the *entire* summer.

"It's time you learned about your New England heritage," Diane's father had said. He'd added, smiling, "And time you got to know your Grandfather Jordan."

They had skirted the real reason Diane was going to Maine for the summer—her mother was scheduled to have a serious operation. It would be better, too, for Diane to be out of the hot city, her father had said, but she knew the real reason was that it would make things easier for her mother. She understood it was for the best, but still she couldn't help feeling left out.

Since her parents had said that though Whale's Creek

was beautiful, it was extremely isolated, Diane had been delighted to discover that Bruce was ten; Darryl, twelve; and Spider, eleven—exactly her own age. But it didn't take her long to find out that the boys didn't give one straw about *her*. The three Whale's Creek Ghosts climbed trees, played ball, and fished in the creek. Every night at dusk they raced in the apple orchard, playing a game called Galloping Ghost—and they didn't want company.

They made it clear that Diane was an intruder, and that a girl would be just so much excess baggage. Furthermore, Diane was "from away." Even though her father had been brought up in Whale's Creek, and her grandfather had lived there all his life, *she* was an outsider.

Diane couldn't understand it. She'd thought that the boys would welcome a new neighbor. Perhaps, she speculated, it was because she was small for her age. But if she could prove that she could do everything they did, maybe then they'd invite her to be a Whale's Creek Ghost.

"A girl!" Darryl had hooted. "No girls allowed in *our* club."

"We don't let just anyone join," Bruce had said.

"Besides, you have to pass a test before you can become a Ghost," Spider had added.

"But I can do everything you can," Diane had protested, with hurt feelings.

"Can you swim?" Bruce had asked her. "There's no ocean in Missouri."

"Of course I can swim," Diane had retorted. "Better than you can!"

That fib, Diane thought now, had been the worst possible mistake. She couldn't swim a stroke. Until today it hadn't mattered, because the weather had been too chilly even to stick a toe in the ocean. But today, the day of the annual Lobster Picnic, everyone went swimming after the feast—no matter how cold the weather. Diane shuddered. She had botched everything with her lie. Now she wouldn't stand a chance of becoming a Whale's Creek Ghost—not after the boys discovered that she couldn't swim at all!

"Diane?" Grandfather appeared in the doorway between the shop and the workroom. He was tall, yet round, had snowy white hair parted in the middle, and wore eyeglasses that were always slipping down on his nose. "Suppose it's time to close up shop?" he asked.

Diane smiled. "It's eleven o'clock. Your time . . ."

"Let's see . . ." Grandfather Jordan frowned. "That would make it . . ." He chuckled and gave up. "About time to get ready, I should think."

Diane laughed as her grandfather disappeared into the workroom. Because he didn't bother to set his clocks back in the fall or ahead in the spring, Grandfather Jordan never knew the exact time so he was always an hour earlier or an hour later than everyone else in Whale's

Creek. "A jolly individualist," Diane's father had de-
scribed Grandfather. "You'll like him." Diane smiled
and thought that her father had been absolutely right
about both things.

"Why don't you go along to the house and get into
your bathing suit?" Grandfather called from the workroom. "I'll be there shortly."

"All right," Diane called back. The bell tinkled as she
closed the front door to the shop. Above the door, a
faded sign creaked in the breeze. It read, "Shaw Jordan,
Potter," in very dim letters. When Diane had offered
to help her grandfather repaint the sign, he'd chuckled.
"No need of that," he had told her. "Might invite too
much business that way."

Disconsolate as she felt, Diane had to smile. With
Bugle, she walked up the path beside the pottery to
Grandfather's neat white house. Upstairs in her cosy
bedroom, with the sloping ceiling and gabled windows,
she sat down on the bed, and the beagle curled up on the
rainbow-colored rag rug on the floor. From one window,
Diane could see the Appleton farm; from the other, a
bit of blue ocean beyond the meadow. But no matter how
she tried, she couldn't forget what was coming. When
the Whale's Creek Ghosts found out that she couldn't
swim, she might just as well forget about them for the
rest of her stay with Grandfather.

Diane flipped a braid back over her shoulder. Though
this was the busy season at the pottery, Grandfather had

done his best to make her visit fun. Almost every evening they walked along the shore with Bugle, her grandfather pointing out Shelter Island Light, and the other islands in the bay. "The sea is good company," Grandfather often said.

But Diane didn't agree, and she thought Whale's Creek was the loneliest place in the world. The vast ocean dwarfed everything, and made her feel lost and homesick. On foggy days, the sea looked frightening, and horns blew hoarsely and continuously. On those days, she worried even more about her mother, and St. Louis seemed a million miles away.

Today was one of those lonely days, Diane thought. For two weeks, she'd knocked herself out to show Darryl, Spider, and Bruce that she could do everything they did. She wanted so much to be included in the boys' fun that she'd done every single thing they wanted to do, and agreed with every single thing they said. "Ditto" was what they called her now, instead of Diane.

"Me, too," she had fallen into the habit of saying. She'd even admired Spider's unlovely collection of insects—and she hated crawling things. When Darryl said, "I'd give my eyeteeth for a boat, just any old boat, so we could go fishing," Diane echoed, "Ditto." She'd never fished in her life, and she despised worms.

Downstairs, the kitchen door opened, and Diane heard Grandfather Jordan washing his hands at the sink. There was no putting it off any longer. She climbed out of her faded blue dungarees and into a bathing suit, and her grandfather was waiting when she plodded downstairs.

With Bugle scampering ahead, they walked along the path through the apple orchard and across the meadow to the shore. Daisies, devil's-paintbrush, and buttercups dressed the green meadow in gay summer colors. From the shore came the tangy smell of seaweed at low tide.

"Won't want to swim for a while," Grandfather said. "Not until the tide comes in, at least. Too many sea urchins at low tide, and if you get those spines in your foot, you'll be all night getting the pesky things out."

No swimming? A reprieve? Diane almost danced the rest of the way to the beach. Bright-colored lobster buoys bobbed in the water close to the creek, and at the other end of the beach, a crowd was gathered near fires which crackled under giant black pots.

"Perhaps they can use an extra hand," Grandfather said, and he headed toward the far end of the beach.

Diane scrambled over barnacle-covered rocks to where Darryl, Spider, and Bruce were struggling to launch some boards they had nailed together into a makeshift raft. Spider had skidded on wet seaweed and was knee-deep in the cold water.

"If we had a real boat," he complained, "we wouldn't have to fool around like this."

"Hi, Ditto . . ." Darryl nodded, and tried to retrieve the raft which was floating out of reach.

"I quit!" Disgusted, Bruce turned to Diane. "What have you got?"

She held out a green sea urchin that she'd found stranded on the rocks.

"I'd hate to step on one of those," Spider said.

"Ditto," Diane agreed. A starfish clung to a rock just below the water, and she stooped to pick it up.

"Ugly-looking thing." Darryl turned up his nose.

Though Diane would have liked to look more closely at the purplish starfish, she put it back into the water.

"Wish those lobsters would hurry and get cooked," said Spider.

"Me, too." The words were barely out of Diane's mouth when a shout, "Lobsters ready!" started a race toward the steaming pots.

After lobsters and blueberry pie, nearly everyone lazed around on the beach. Rusty Babson, a young red-haired lobsterman who sometimes played chess with Grandfather Jordan, organized a baseball game. There were also volley ball and badminton games going on in the meadow. Diane and her grandfather were playing badminton against Bruce Eaton and his father when Spider called out from the shore.

"Come on," he yelled. "The tide's in enough to swim from the dock."

"Soon as this game's over," Bruce shouted back.

The butterflies in Diane's stomach whirled almost as

fast as the badminton birdie. Swimming! So she hadn't escaped, after all.

"Come on, Ditto." Bruce challenged her the second the badminton game ended. "Now you can show us how they swim in Missouri."

The only thing she was about to show was that she was a big liar, Diane thought grimly. Postponing the humiliation for as long as possible, she scuffed slowly toward the beach.

"Last one in is a rotten apple!" Darryl yelled. He dove into the water, and the other two boys plunged in after him.

Diane walked along the runway and was standing on the dock when Spider climbed back up the ladder. "Well, look who's the rotten apple—Ditto!" He looked at Diane and grinned. "Jump or be pushed," he threatened.

Diane stood at the edge of the dock and stared down at the water.

"Jump or be pushed!" Spider repeated.

Frantically, Diane eyed the water and then the boys. They were waiting, all three of them. There was no way out. With a despairing look, she held her nose and jumped feet first into the chilly blue ocean.

2 ❧ Follow-the-Leader

Sputtering and struggling, her mouth filled with salt water, Diane bobbed to the surface too far from the dock to reach it. Desperately she thrashed her arms and legs. If she ever got to the dock, she would never, never again tell a fib, she promised herself fervently. The ladder was almost within her grasp and then, miraculously, her hand was on it. Shaking, she climbed up onto the dock.

"Too cold for you?" Spider grinned.

Diane could only nod. Before her knees buckled, she sat down on the sun-washed dock. It had been a close call, but somehow the boys weren't aware of it. They horsed around on the dock, yelling and pushing one another into the water.

"Race you to the beach!" Darryl cried.

Diane's "Me, too" was missing. She didn't intend to tempt fate again; she'd walk along the runway to the shore. When the boys dove into the water, she stayed put on the dock. Once had been enough—it had almost been too much. For the rest of the afternoon, she was a watcher, and a very silent one.

That night at supper, Diane asked her grandfather if he knew how to swim. He shook his head. "Never even tried to learn," he said.

"Me, either," Diane murmured.

Grandfather Jordan looked surprised. "But you were in the water with the boys this afternoon . . ."

She flushed. "I—I told them I could swim."

"Oh." Grandfather looked at her. "Your tongue wrapped itself around the wrong words? Well," he continued, "it's not much fun to be at the shore if you can't swim. In view of that, perhaps we'd both better do some learning. They say you can't teach an old dog new tricks, but *they* are inclined to spread all kinds of rumors."

After lunch the next day, Grandfather, declaring time out for a visit to Whale's Neck, closed up the pottery. They were in the kitchen ready to leave when Diane noticed that Bugle was missing. Grandfather shook his head. "That beagle must be off chasing rabbits again." Diane giggled, because she knew what was coming. Her grandfather reached for the bugle hanging by the kitchen door, and from the back steps he vigorously blew a series of notes. The call echoed over Whale's Creek and soon Bugle appeared, wagging his stubby tail. "Fool dog only answers to chow call," Grandfather Jordan grumbled.

"I think he's pretty smart," Diane said, laughing.

Grandfather smiled as he gave the beagle a dog biscuit. "You may be right," he agreed.

In the green pickup that Grandfather relied on for transportation, they drove the four miles into Whale's Neck. Bugle sat up front in the middle, not missing a thing, and he didn't budge when they parked on Main Street.

"Here we are," Grandfather said, "right in the heart of downtown Whale's Neck."

Diane laughed. The village didn't look much like downtown St. Louis, but then, almost everything about Maine was different from Missouri. The shops, one of each kind, were clustered about a common on which stood a white church. At the foot of Main Street were the waterfront and harbor—the bustling section of Whale's Neck.

In the small library, Grandfather introduced Diane to Miss Perkins, the librarian, and asked for a book that would teach them to swim.

"You intend to take it up, too, Mr. Jordan?" The librarian looked startled.

"Certainly do, Lily," Grandfather declared. "Would you like to come along with us?"

Miss Perkins stammered, blushed, and guessed she would take a rain check. She hurried to find their book.

Outside the library again, Grandfather Jordan said, "Now, why do you suppose Lily Perkins was so all-fired surprised that I intend to learn to swim?"

"I can't imagine," Diane replied, stifling a giggle.

Their progress along Main Street was slow. Everyone they met stopped to chat. As they were exiting from the drugstore with ice-cream cones, they saw the three Whale's Creek Ghosts.

"Hi!" Diane cried eagerly.

"Hi, Ditto." Darryl sounded indifferent.

"We're just on the way home, boys," said Grandfather. "Would you like a ride?"

"Oh, yes, thanks," they chorused.

The boys jumped into the back of the pickup. When Grandfather stopped at the Appleton farm, they leaped out noisily. "Thanks again, Mr. Jordan," Darryl called.

Diane stuck her head out of the window. She couldn't keep the longing out of her voice. "What are you doing this afternoon?" she asked.

Darryl shrugged. "Guess we'll be busy."

Diane missed the wink Spider gave his brother before he said, "If Ditto wants to be a Whale's Creek Ghost, maybe we'd better find out whether she's a good sport."

Darryl looked suddenly interested. "OK," he said. "Want to stay, Ditto?"

"May I?" Diane begged her grandfather.

"Don't see why not." Grandfather smiled as she hopped out of the pickup. He shifted gears and waved. "Have a good time."

"What are we going to do?" Diane asked the boys.

"How about Follow-the-Leader?" suggested Spider. "First dibs on leader," he added.

"OK," the other two boys agreed.

Darryl explained the game to Diane. "Simple," he said. "We follow Spider and do exactly what he does."

That she could do, Diane thought.

"Let's go," Spider said, and started running. With Bruce and Darryl right behind him, he dodged into the pine grove beside the farm, and Diane had trouble keeping up. Were they trying to run away from her? she wondered. Could that be the game? Determined not to let them out of sight, she raced after them.

The three came out of the pine grove and streaked toward the Appletons' red barn; Spider darted into the barn, with Darryl and Bruce close behind him. When Diane reached the barn, it took her eyes a minute to adjust to the darkness. Then she saw Bruce go through an open window at the back of the barn. She rushed to the window, climbed up on the low sill, and jumped out after the others. To her dismay, she landed and began to sink into something soft, squashy, and very smelly.

3 ❦ The Tree House

The three boys hooted with laughter, as they held their noses and pointed at Diane. "Next time, look before you leap!" Darryl almost choked on the words. "You didn't jump *out* far enough."

Stiffly, Diane picked herself out of the manure pile. Then she turned and ran. Her face contorted with the effort to hold back tears, she cut through the apple orchard and sped around to the back of the pottery. There she paused, tears now streaming down her face. Could she reach the house without running into her grandfather? She didn't want to see *anyone*. Too late, she noticed that the back door of the pottery was open.

Grandfather Jordan stepped outside. He was shaking bits of clay from his huge work apron when he looked up and saw Diane. "Home so soon?" he asked in surprise. Then he took a second look. Without a word he led her, sobbing, up to the back of the house. Here he attached the hose to the faucet. "Hold your breath," he warned her. "This is going to be cold."

The first blast shocked Diane out of her weeping, and by the time her grandfather had finished the clean-up job, she was smiling weakly. He put the hose away, then knelt in his garden to retie some tomato plants. Diane sat on the patio to dry off in the sun.

The bell at the pottery tinkled. "Customer," she murmured.

"They'll be back if they want anything." Placidly, Grandfather continued working on the tomato plants. Then he said in a quiet voice, "How did you get into such a mess?"

Thinking about what the boys had done, Diane almost started crying again. "Well . . ." she began, and then stumbled through the whole story.

Her grandfather frowned. "That was an unkind thing for them to do."

"It—it was a test," she explained, "to find out

whether I'm a good enough sport to be a Whale's Creek Ghost."

"They might have thought up a better kind of test. I'm not altogether sure I'd want to belong to their club."

"But I do," Diane blurted. "They have such a good time, and . . ." She stopped.

Her grandfather nodded. "Whale's Creek can't be too lively with just an antique potter for company."

"I didn't mean that. You're not an antique!"

"Pretty close to it." Grandfather Jordan grinned. "Now let's attack this problem scientifically. That is, if you're positive you want to join that club."

"I do!"

"Well," he said, "the same mysterious *they* claim that if you build a better mousetrap, the world will beat a path to your door."

"I don't think the boys are interested in mousetraps." Diane smiled.

"What does interest them?" he asked.

"More than anything, they want a boat."

Grandfather shook his head. "That would appear to be outside the realm of possibility."

"They've been talking about a clubhouse," she offered.

"There's an idea."

"What about a tree house? In the orchard."

"That's not so farfetched." Grandfather nodded. "There's plenty of lumber in the shed."

"If I built a tree house and they wanted it for a club-

house, then they'd have to let me join, wouldn't they?"
Diane asked.

"Sounds reasonable. Tell you what—I'll give you a
hand after I'm through at the pottery this afternoon."

He went back to the shop, and after looking at the
lumber in the shed, Diane decided there was more than
enough for a tree house. In the orchard, she picked out
a good-sized apple tree with nicely forked branches.
Why not tackle the project now? When Grandfather got
through work, she'd already have made a good start on
the tree house.

With Bugle at her heels, she dragged a stepladder
from the shed to the orchard. Then she returned for a
hammer and nails. It was hot work, and by the time she'd
finished lugging a pile of boards to the orchard, her face
was streaked with dirt and sweat.

"Whew!" She sat down on a stump and mopped her
face. Building a tree house wasn't really a good way to
spend a sweltering summer afternoon. She'd much rather
be wading in the creek. But if she built a good tree house,
the boys would certainly welcome her into their club. Diane sighed and tried to keep that in mind as she debated
how to begin the project.

Struggling, she got one board up into the fork of the
apple tree. With difficulty, she hoisted the second board
alongside the first; then, clutching the hammer and nails,
she shinnied awkwardly up the tree.

"Ouch!" A sliver from one of the boards dug into the

palm of her hand. She tried to get it out, but the sliver was imbedded too deeply.

The special whistle of the Whale's Creek Ghosts pierced the orchard, and Diane groaned. The boys—and she'd wanted to keep the tree house a secret until it was finished. Perhaps they wouldn't see her. She tried to settle herself inconspicuously in the tree, and as she did so, the loose boards began to slide out of place. When she grabbed frantically for them, the hammer and nails sailed to the ground, and, noisily, the boards followed. Then, with Bugle barking like crazy, Diane herself pitched out of the apple tree.

The three Whale's Creek Ghosts crowded around her. "Are you OK, Ditto?" Darryl actually looked worried.

The wind knocked right out of her, Diane lay flat on her back. Gingerly she moved her arms and legs. "I—I guess so."

The boys helped her up, but the minute they discovered she was still in one piece, their attitude changed.

"What were you doing in that apple tree?" Spider demanded.

Diane didn't answer. She was furious at herself for falling out of the tree and ruining the surprise.

Darryl glanced at the hammer, nails, and boards. "You weren't planning to build a tree house, were you?"

Bruce laughed. "A *girl* building a tree house?"

"What do you know? Ditto's dotty!" Spider grinned.

Diane bit her tongue. She wanted to retort tha
could build a better tree house than they could, but she
knew it would be a mistake to say that.

Darryl eyed the forked branches of the apple tree.
"Might not be such a bad idea. Might make a good clubhouse."

The boys looked over the tree, debating about the
merits of a tree house. "Could even build two levels,"
Darryl speculated.

"Let's get going!" Spider grabbed the hammer, and
Bruce picked up a board.

"Why don't we build a ladder, too," Diane suggested.
"It would be easier to climb up and down."

The boys stared. "Sorry," Darryl said, "no girls allowed." **U. S. 1442357**

"What!" Diane could hardly believe her ears. The
tree house had been her idea, her project, and now the
Ghosts were taking it over—lock, stock, and barrel.
It wasn't fair!

"No girls allowed," Darryl repeated, and the boys
started nailing boards together as if she weren't even
there.

Diane glared at them; then she turned on her heel
and left. They had taken over her tree house and ruled
her out. They had no intention at all of inviting her to
join their club. She had wasted an entire afternoon on
something she hadn't really wanted to do. And what had
come of it? Nothing.

At supper, she told Grandfather what had happened. "Can't you do something about the boys?" she wailed. "It's your apple tree and your lumber. Can't you stop them from building the tree house?"

"Could," Grandfather admitted, "but it might not be the best procedure if you still want to get into that club. Would only lessen your chances. Might turn the boys against you for good."

In spite of her feelings, Diane reluctantly agreed with him.

"Never mind," he said, "we'll think of something else."

That evening, Grandfather had work to do at the pottery, so Diane wandered over the meadow with Bugle. By the seashore, she sat down on a rock. From the orchard there came the sweet smell of apple trees, and the sounds of sawing and hammering on the tree house. It made her feel even worse to think that the lumber the boys were using belonged to her grandfather.

The sun went down, the boys went home, and still Diane sat by the sea, gazing at Shelter Island Light as it flashed its warning. Whale's Creek might be beautiful, but it was the most desolate place in the world. How much she wished she were back in Missouri! She'd give anything to be home, but there was a long, lonely summer to get through first.

When darkness set in, Diane stood up. Grandfather would be finished at the pottery. In the cloudy, moonless night, the lobster buoys floated darkly by the creek. Then she saw a tiny light. At first, it seemed to be on top of the water, then underneath, and then it disappeared altogether. An odd time for a lobsterman to be checking his traps, she thought. What's more, she didn't see any boat. Perhaps she had simply imagined the small, shifting light. Shrugging, Diane plodded home.

4 ❧ Ghostly Business

No longer did the three boys build rafts at the beach; now, from dawn to dusk, they worked on the tree house. Diane watched their progress from a distance. The tree house had turned into a complicated thing, with two levels and, as she had suggested, a ladder which they could pull up behind them.

In the late afternoons, Grandfather Jordan and Diane went to the creek and worked on their swimming. Grandfather, in his old-fashioned bathing suit, guessed he wouldn't win any beauty contests. "Or swimming contests, either," he added. Diane was feeling more at home in the water, and Grandfather pronounced her dog-paddle, "Pretty fair."

Wistfully, Diane watched the boys. She had almost decided to give up on the Ghosts and their club when a long letter arrived from St. Louis. Her mother would be hospitalized longer than expected, Daddy wrote. Though she was coming along nicely, and Diane was not to worry, the recovery was quite slow. Diane could read between the lines. She would have to stay in Whale's Creek for the entire depressing and lonely summer.

If only she had someone to talk to, someone to confide in, the summer would be so much easier. She couldn't worry her mother by telling her how she felt about Maine, and she wouldn't hurt Grandfather Jordan's feelings for the world. Moping, she came to a decision. Since she was now definitely stuck in Whale's Creek, just once more, one last time, she'd try to convince the Ghosts that she'd be an asset to their club.

"The way to a man's heart is through his stomach," Grandfather suggested. "Or it was supposed to be in the old days."

One hot day, Diane stayed in the kitchen baking cookies. The first batch burned, and the second wasn't baked long enough. Stubbornly she kept going, and finally one batch turned out just right—crispy and tasty. Carrying a tray with the cookies on a paper plate, cups, and a pitcher of lemonade, Diane made her way to the tree house, past large signs that said, "Stay Out," "No Trespassing," and "No Girls Allowed."

High in the tree house, Darryl looked down at her. "Can't you read?" he demanded.

Spotting the cookies, Spider climbed down the ladder. "Tea time," he squeaked.

The other two boys were quick to follow Spider down the ladder. "Hi, Ditto," Bruce greeted her.

Diane smiled. "How about a lemonade break?" She'd barely set down the tray when every last cookie was gone from the plate, and the lemonade pitcher was drained dry.

"Thanks, Ditto," the boys chorused. Quickly they retreated into their tree house, dragging the ladder up behind them.

Below, Diane stared up at them. They hadn't waited, suggested that she join them, or left even one cookie for her—and after she'd spent those long, hot hours over the stove, making the treat for them. Snatching up the tray, she marched out of the orchard. It was the very *last time* she would try to impress the Whale's Creek Ghosts.

"Grandfather," she said as they were fixing supper that night, "perhaps I ought to find out exactly what kind of good sports the Ghosts are—the way they did with me. What do you think?"

Her grandfather smiled. "Sounds fair enough. What did you have in mind?"

Diane giggled. "The boys play Galloping Ghost every night in the orchard. What if they ran into another ghost? An extra one, all dressed in white."

This time, Grandfather laughed heartily. "I'm almost certain there's an old sheet in the linen closet. Let's take a look."

At dusk, as usual, they heard the boys beginning their game. Diane cut eyeholes in the sheet so she could see, and Grandfather nodded his approval. "A small ghost," he said, "but effective."

The minute it was dark, Diane stole out of the back door. There was no moon, and she wished that she'd brought a flashlight, as Grandfather had suggested. The special whistle of the Whale's Creek Ghosts shrilled through the orchard, and though she stealthily crept toward the sound, it seemed to stay the same distance away. She kept stumbling through the orchard, but she suspected that the boys were on their way home. To make sure, she walked to the top of the meadow. The lights were all on at the Appleton farm, and it was dead quiet in Whale's Creek. The three Ghosts had quit for the night.

Ruefully, Diane thought that she had been a failure—again. Below the meadow, waves lapped high up on the beach, and Shelter Island Light signaled with its blinking beacon. Diane sighed. Nothing much changed in Whale's Creek; nothing much happened, either. Around the lobster buoys, a light seemed to play, then was gone. It was, she decided, simply a reflection in the water.

At home, Diane found Grandfather Jordan playing chess with Rusty Babson. "I'm a flop as a ghost," she told them, "but I did see a funny little light around the lobster buoys at the creek."

Rusty looked up from the chessboard. "A light?"

Diane nodded. "It must have been a reflection, because it disappeared."

"Any boats around?" he asked.

"No." She shook her head.

"Might have been phosphorus," Grandfather offered. "Or perhaps the German spies are back."

"Spies!" Diane exclaimed.

"Spies," he repeated.

"In Whale's Creek?"

"Well, not right in Whale's Creek," Grandfather amended, "but up the coast a way—beyond Whale's Neck."

"Was that the War of 1812?" Rusty grinned.

"Now, I'm not *that* old. No, it was during World War II, and I remember it plain as day. Summertime it was then, and everyone took his hitch at airplane spotting from the fire tower in the hill back of Whale's Neck. Your father was small at the time." Grandfather smiled at Diane. "He used to keep me company on the Thursday afternoon shift."

"But what about the *spies?*" she pleaded.

"Oh, yes." Grandfather would not be hurried. "Along with spotting airplanes, we were supposed to keep an eye on the bay and report anything in the least suspicious. Submarines were what everyone was worried about. In those days," he added, "you couldn't even sail in the harbor without carrying along an official identification card with your picture on it. Had to travel all the way to the Coast Guard Station in Southwest Harbor to get one."

"The spies," Diane begged.

"I'm coming to that," said her grandfather. "After a while, the airplane- and submarine-watching got to be kind of a joke. 'How many enemy planes did you report today?' your grandmother would ask me. Of course, along with the other ladies, she kept right on rolling bandages and knitting for the soldiers and, though it was considered a mite foolish, the men stuck to watching from the fire tower. We miscalculated a bit, but then, the Germans did, too."

"Yes?" prodded Diane.

"Early one morning, when everyone was still sleeping, a foreign submarine put two men adrift on a raft. They landed on a small beach above Whale's Neck, and began walking along the road to town." Grandfather started to smile.

"What happened?"

"Well, those two Germans must have been somewhat misinformed as to Maine's climate," Grandfather said, "because they were bundled up in coats and hats heavy enough for the North Pole. They got as far as the outskirts of town when Sheriff Higgins came along in the patrol car."

"What did he do?" Diane asked.

"He just hustled them right into his car and off to the county jail."

"But how did he know they were spies?"

"Sheriff's no dummy," Grandfather Jordan answered. "Besides, it wasn't too hard to deduce that something was mighty queer."

"Guess not," Rusty remarked. "Two bundled-up strangers walking along the road first thing on a summer morning are bound to attract attention in Whale's Neck."

"All that excitement here?" Diane murmured. "I can't believe it."

"It's the gospel truth," said Grandfather.

Rusty nodded. "I can back you up—my father's told that same story many times."

"After that, no one joshed about the airplane and submarine spotting, and we all kept sharper eyes on the sea and the sky," Grandfather Jordan said.

Diane listened in silence. She found it hard to imagine

that anything so exciting could have happened in this desolate and lonely part of Maine.

Cloudy, rainy weather set in, and Diane did her best to keep busy. She tried the potter's wheel, but with small success. Though Grandfather stood by with patient instructions, the clay kept falling apart in her unskilled hands. Whenever the rain let up, Grandfather Jordan showed her how to dig clams—how to drop a rock on the beach when the tide was out and then watch for the telltale squirt of water that indicated a clam hidden under the sand. He also pointed out the tide pools, and some of the sea things living in them, and at low tide he let Diane help him dig clay for the pottery from the shore.

On the next clear night, Diane dug out her ghost costume again. When she heard the boys playing Galloping Ghost in the orchard, she put on the sheet and slipped out of the house. This time she took along a small flashlight, just in case she might need it. She stole through the orchard in the direction of the boys' whistles. Cautiously, she edged closer until she could see all three of the Whale's Creek Ghosts together near the tree house. She was ready to jump out with a loud, scary "Whoo!" when behind her a twig snapped.

Diane whirled. She didn't need her little flashlight to see the huge white ghost, flapping its arms directly in back of her. With a startled gasp, Diane turned and ran out of the orchard, and she could hear the boys noisily retreating in the other direction. Running, stumbling, Diane raced for home.

5 ❦ "Bail!"

Diane ran through the open back door. "Grandfather!"
she cried. There was no answer—not one sound. Her
heart still thudding, she looked out of the window.
There were no lights on at the pottery. Where was
Grandfather Jordan? What had happened to him? And
who or *what* had been behind her in the orchard?

Peering out of the back door, Diane's heart almost
stopped altogether. Lumbering up the back walk was the
same large ghost she had seen in the orchard.

"Shhh, Diane," whispered the ghost.

"Grandfather!" Diane gasped.

Grandfather Jordan struggled out of his sheet. Sheepishly, he looked at her. "I didn't mean to scare you to death. After you left, the thought crossed my mind that if, as *they* say, two heads are better than one, perhaps two ghosts would be better than one."

They looked at each other, and then burst out laughing.

"It didn't turn out quite as I'd anticipated," Grandfather said, "and I only hope the Whale's Creek Ghosts didn't recognize me. It's a bit unusual for an elderly potter to run around at night all dressed up in a sheet."

"That's the best kind of grandfather to have," Diane insisted, giggling.

After they had hot chocolate, Grandfather said it was time for all good ghosts to go to bed—and keep a vow of silence about the escapade. They would have to devise another, better way of testing whether the boys were good sports.

Diane thought that she didn't even want to do that any more. If the Whale's Creek Ghosts weren't interested in her, then she wasn't interested in them. More and more she resented the nickname they had given her. "Ditto" was no compliment. She didn't want to be exactly like the boys; she didn't want to be a carbon copy of *anyone*. It had been a mistake to try to imitate the boys. If they didn't like her the way she was, then she'd just get along without them. There were other things to do, anyhow.

At her grandfather's suggestion, Diane took over the job of digging clay for the pottery. This was done at low tide, of course, and Bugle was always at her heels. On clear days at the beach she could see Mt. Desert Island rising from the sea. She was beginning to love the shore and the islands in the bay in the early morning stillness. To her surprise, she found that the sea was not so lonely, after all. Something was always happening on the water. All kinds of boats passed Whale's Creek, and the sturdy, booted lobstermen waved to her as they pulled up their traps. Rusty Babson occasionally stopped for a few minutes' chat.

There were small things from the sea to be found in the watery crevices of the rocks, and one morning Diane became intrigued by a large tide pool. The longer she watched, the more things, moving and still, she found. Deciding to start a collection of Maine shells to take back to Missouri, she drew a snail out of the pool and set it on a rock. Gingerly, she picked out a green sea urchin, examined its sharp spines, and put it beside the snail.

To her astonishment, the snail suddenly began to scuttle away sideways. A snail couldn't do that, she thought. As she watched, a small crab wriggled out of the snail's shell and raced madly across the rock. Diane laughed. The crab had chosen the snail's empty shell as a hiding place!

The special whistle of the Whale's Creek Ghosts floated down to the shore before Diane saw the boys. Bugle barked, then settled back with his nose on a rock as the Ghosts appeared, dragging their latest boat contraption along the beach.

"Hi, Ditto," Darryl grunted in her general direction.

Diane just nodded. The boys carried fishing lines and cans of worms. Of course, they didn't invite her to join them, but even if they had, she would have refused. The thought of sticking a worm on a fishhook sent shivers up her spine.

Pushing and pulling, the boys got their homemade boat into the creek, and then climbed aboard with their fishing paraphernalia. By the time they had poled the craft to the middle of the creek, water was pouring through the seams.

"Hurry!" they shouted to one another. "Bail!"

From the beach, Diane watched the confusion. At first, the boys tried to get the water out of the boat with their cupped hands; then they dumped the worms over the side and used the cans to bail. To keep the craft afloat, one of the boys had to bail constantly. Across the water, Diane could hear their whispers.

"What do you say we ask Ditto to come?"

"Why not?"

"We could fish—and she could bail!"

Diane almost giggled aloud. A few days ago she would have jumped at the chance to be with the Ghosts, but not now. She didn't like to fish, she didn't like worms, she didn't like to bail, and she wasn't going to pretend that she did. Not any more.

"Say, Ditto . . ." Spider cleared his throat. "Want to come with us?"

Diane shook her head. "No, thanks," she called back politely.

There was surprised silence from the boys. Then Darryl tried. "Come on," he invited.

"Yes, come on," Bruce chimed in.

"Sorry. My grandfather needs some clay for the pottery." Diane stood up, holding the shells and the bucket of clay. "Besides, I don't like to fish. Or *bail*, either." Then, with Bugle beside her, she walked up the beach without a backward glance.

6 ❦ In a Jam

After depositing the bucket of clay at the pottery, Diane showed Grandfather Jordan the sea urchin, and told him about the crab that had been inside the snail's shell.

"Probably a hermit crab," Grandfather said. "They're fond of borrowing other people's houses."

"I'd like to start a collection," she told him. "It would be fun to show my friends in Missouri the kinds of shells we have in Maine."

Noticing her use of the word "we," Grandfather smiled. "Why don't you use a shelf in the workroom for your collection? Then at the end of the summer, we can pack everything in a carton and send it to Missouri." He told Diane how to clean the shells, and explained that, after it had dried out, the sea urchin's spines would fall off, and only a thin, fragile shell would remain. "Of course, the best time for gathering shells is at dead low tide after a storm. On our next trip to Whale's Neck, we'll pick up a tide table and a book about shells from Lily Perkins at the library."

Diane hurried back to the shore with a basket. The tide was coming in rapidly, the boys had gone, and she guessed they had grown weary of bailing. Walking along the beach, looking for shells, Diane saw things she'd never noticed before. At the end of the morning, she carried back a basketful of shells and a weathered, silvery piece of driftwood that Grandfather said would be a lovely decoration for the pottery.

After one look outside on Friday morning, Grandfather Jordan closed up shop. "Picnic lunch is in order," he declared.

Bugle jumped into the green pickup with them, and they headed for Whale's Neck. Saying, "Nothing like a surprise to brighten a day," Grandfather kept their final destination a secret.

At the wharf in Whale's Neck, they looked up a Captain Richards. "Got a couple of passengers this morning," Grandfather told the captain. "No, three," he amended, with a glance at Bugle.

"Glad to have you aboard!" the captain boomed. "The *Nellie G.* is due to leave in five minutes."

Diane was overjoyed. On this clear, crisp day, nothing could be more perfect than going in the mail boat with Captain Richards on his rounds of the islands. A seasoned sea dog, Bugle leaped onto the *Nellie G.* and settled himself comfortably on top of the cabin.

Except for a sailboat or two in the distance, and some lobstermen heading for their traps, there were few boats beyond Whale's Neck Harbor. Through Captain Richards' binoculars, Diane marveled at magnificent Mt. Desert, and she wondered how the early explorers felt upon sighting the island for the first time. They must have been overwhelmed at the beauty of the mountains towering above the sea.

"Look! Porpoises!" Captain Richards pointed them out, diving and playing in the bay. And a little farther on they glimpsed some seals.

The first stops for the mail boat were at the closer, more populated islands. After that, they headed for the scattered, sparsely settled isles where the air was chilly even on a warm summer's day. At Butternut Island, the three passengers went ashore.

"Be back for you in a couple of hours," Captain Richards promised.

At a small store at the landing, they bought soda to go with their picnic lunch. Then they walked past the smattering of houses clustered by the shore and up the hill to the summit, where there was a lovely view of the islands in the bay. After their picnic lunch and some sweet-tasting wild raspberries they picked for dessert, they ambled down to the sea and found the beach covered with round, smooth, surf-pounded stones. Though Bugle refused to stick in even one paw, Diane waded in the cold water. They collected a few of the small flat sea urchins called sand dollars, and some unusual and vividly colored stones that were not to be found on the mainland.

On the rolling trip home in the *Nellie G.,* Captain Richards nodded at the black thunderheads forming in the west. "I'm afraid there's a storm coming up," he reported.

"Guess our last surprise of the day will be a damp one," Grandfather said. "The Appletons have invited us for supper, but I suspect the cookout will turn into a 'cook in.' "

Though Diane was hardly pleased at the prospect of seeing the boys, she tried to look happy. It had been a wonderful day, and she hated to have it spoiled by the Whale's Creek Ghosts.

Back home, though tired, windblown, and sunburned, they changed from their seafaring outfits into clothes more suitable for supper at the Appletons'. As a gift for Mrs. Appleton, Grandfather Jordan wrapped in tissue a pottery sugar bowl and creamer in the soft blue-gray color that was Diane's favorite.

"I'd like to take something, too," she said.

It was raining too hard to pick any roses, so Grandfather suggested taking along one of the sand dollars from Butternut Island. Diane chose the prettiest one from her collection, and they drove to the neighboring farm.

Mrs. Appleton was thrilled with the sand dollar. "I haven't been to Butternut in years," she said, "and haven't seen one of these lovely things in ages."

Even Spider, Darryl, and Bruce—who was also a guest—were interested, and they examined the sand dollar for some time before Mrs. Appleton set it carefully on the kitchen shelf.

When dinner was over, Grandfather Jordan brought out his harmonica, and they all sang songs until the boys got restless and asked if they could play Sardines, their own version of Hide-and-Seek.

"You go ahead, too, Diane." Mrs. Appleton gave the boys a meaningful look.

"Well, I suppose it's more fun with four," Darryl conceded.

In unison, the three boys shouted, "IT!" To settle

the argument, Grandfather Jordan flipped a coin, and Diane turned out to be the winner of the toss.

"We'll stay downstairs and count to one hundred," Spider explained to her. "You hide upstairs, and then we'll try to find you. The first person to discover the hiding place crawls in and hides, too. Last one to find the place is IT the next time."

Upstairs in the roomy farmhouse, Diane searched for a good place to hide, while downstairs in the kitchen, the boys counted out loud. She opened a door in the upstairs hall and found that it was a huge linen closet, with a pile of quilts on one side of it. Shoving the quilts aside, Diane closed the door and felt her way around in the dark.

"Ready or not—here we come!" the boys yelled from below.

As they tramped up the stairs, Diane burrowed under the quilts, and there she discovered a small opening. Probably a laundry chute, she guessed. Sitting on the edge, she put her feet as far as possible down the chute. She was sure the opening was too small to fall through.

When someone opened the door to the linen closet, Diane squeezed farther into the opening and held her breath. Then the door closed and there was silence. Cramped and hot under the quilts, she decided it was safe to come up for a breath of air. Trying to push aside the quilts over her head, she slipped even farther down the laundry chute. More and more uncomfortable, she tried to move her legs—and couldn't! No matter how she squirmed, it was impossible to get herself out of the opening. Shaken, and a little panicky, Diane realized that she was stuck fast in the Appletons' laundry chute.

7 ❧ An Odd Secret

No matter how she struggled, Diane simply could not get herself free. Instead, she found herself jammed into the laundry chute even more tightly. Now what? she wondered. Her face burning at thoughts of what the boys would say and how they would laugh, she was trying with all her might to get out when the door to the linen closet opened again.

Darryl lifted the quilts and grinned broadly when he

saw Diane. "Well—hello. Move over," he whispered.

Hot and perspiring, Diane gave one last desperate and unsuccessful shove.

"Well, come on," Darryl muttered. "Hurry up."

"I—I can't," she whispered. "I'm stuck."

"You're *what?*"

"Stuck," she repeated miserably.

Darryl started to laugh. "Hey, look everyone," he yelled, "Ditto's stuck in the laundry chute!"

By the time Mr. and Mrs. Appleton and Grandfather Jordan got upstairs, the three boys were already standing around the linen closet, doubled up with laughter. At once, Mr. Appleton put his arms underneath Diane's and eased her up and out of the laundry chute.

When she gulped, "Thank you," her face was red from more than the day's sunburn.

Mr. Appleton glared at the boys. "Why didn't you help Diane instead of standing around and laughing like a bunch of hyenas?"

"You boys should be ashamed of yourselves," Mrs. Appleton scolded. "Why, Diane could have smothered under those quilts! Are you all right, dear?"

"Fine," she mumbled.

Grandfather Jordan rescued her from having to say more by announcing, "Well, we really must leave now. I hate to break up the game, but I've got to get my beauty sleep."

Relieved, Diane found her raincoat, and they said

good-by amid Mrs. Appleton's apologies for her sons' rude behavior. The rain had stopped, and the minute they opened the door at home, Bugle raced out of the house.

"After rabbits again." Grandfather shook his head. "But I can't blow the bugle for that fool dog this late. I might wake Mr. and Mrs. Eaton."

"I'll get Bugle," Diane offered. "I could use a breath of fresh air."

Over the hill, beyond the apple orchard, Bugle was baying loudly and incessantly. "Come here," Diane called. "Come, Bugle!" Since Bugle didn't budge, she crept up behind him and grabbed his collar. Quivering, the dog was looking down at the beach, and Diane was surprised to see a rowboat pulled up on the shore. It was a small, dilapidated rowboat with oars sticking over the side. How did it get there? Who on earth would have left that on the beach? Scooping up Bugle, she hurried home.

When she told her grandfather about the rowboat, he didn't seem alarmed. "Probably belongs to some fisherman," was all he said.

"But would a fisherman have been out in the storm?" she asked.

"We've been gone all day," Grandfather pointed out. "Whoever owns the boat might have left it there when the storm blew up."

Her grandfather was probably right, Diane decided,

though she wondered whether the boat could have been washed ashore in the storm. The boys would be pleased, she thought, if the boat were a stray and didn't belong to anyone. All summer they'd been longing for a boat of their own, and maybe they could have this one.

The next morning Diane and Bugle investigated the beach before breakfast. The shore was deserted, and there was no sign of the rowboat. Rusty Babson waved to her as he hauled up traps by the creek. "Morning," he called.

"Morning, Rusty." She waved back, and walked over to the creek. "Have you lost a rowboat—a dory?" she asked.

"No—why?"

When Diane told him about the decrepit rowboat that had been on the shore the previous evening, the usually smiling Rusty turned serious. "I'd appreciate it if you didn't mention that boat to anyone," he said. "Let's just keep it between the two of us."

"German spies come back?" She laughed.

"Doubt that," Rusty said, "but I'd be happier if we kept that boat a secret."

"OK," Diane agreed, forgetting that she had already told Grandfather about it. Rusty must be joking, she thought. He was teasing her by pretending that something important was going on, when everyone knew that nothing exciting ever happened in Whale's Creek. Watching Rusty pull up his traps and thinking that she'd love to go lobstering before she went back to St. Louis, she spoke up quickly while she still had the courage. "Could I go fishing with you someday?"

Rusty grinned. "Be glad to take you along. One thing, though—you've got to promise not to get seasick."

She laughed. "Cross my heart and hope to die."

"Can't take you today," the young lobsterman said, "but we'll plan it soon."

Diane was delighted. She was sure that Rusty wouldn't forget, and this might be a chance to add some deep-water shells to her collection—shells that couldn't be found along the beach or within wading distance of low tide. Perhaps Grandfather would help her make a dredge, like the one in the book about shells that they had borrowed from the library. Maybe Rusty would let her try it out; they could drag it along behind his boat. If only she had a boat of her own, Diane thought, she could look for deep-water shells anytime she wanted to.

Back at the house, Grandfather was frying bacon, and Diane told him about Rusty's promise to take her lobstering. "Do you think he'd mind if I took along a dredge to pick up shells?" she asked.

"Rusty's pretty good-natured," Grandfather Jordan observed. "Perhaps tonight we could get a start on making that dredge."

Even though Diane suspected that Rusty had only

been joking about keeping the rowboat a secret, she didn't mention to her grandfather that it had been gone this morning. Instead, they talked about the different kinds of shells she might expect to find with the dredge.

The next letter from her mother brought Diane the news that she would be flying home sooner than they had thought. "I'm feeling much stronger now," her mother wrote, "and we can't wait to have you back with us in St. Louis."

Though Grandfather Jordan was happy about her mother's progress, he said ruefully, "I'm going to miss having you *here*."

Unexpectedly, Diane found herself hoping that she wouldn't have to go back to St. Louis right away. It would be a long time before she saw her grandfather again, and she certainly didn't want to miss the lobstering trip with Rusty.

Now that the tree house was finished, curiously enough the Whale's Creek Ghosts seldom went there. Diane saw them often at the beach, launching their homemade rafts or fishing, and she heard them saying how much they wished they had a real boat of their own. Diane wished the same thing. Her shell collection was growing, and she was anxious to add new and different ones that she knew could be found only in deep water.

One morning, walking along the beach and looking for

shells, Diane spotted something—a shell larger than she had ever seen on the shore. Though they were usually found only in deep water, she was sure it was a scallop—and it was *alive*. She picked it up, walked over to where the boys were fishing, and showed it to them.

"It's a scallop, all right," Spider said.

"But I've never seen one on the beach before," added Darryl.

"It could have been washed ashore in a storm," Bruce suggested.

"There wasn't any storm last night," Diane said, "and I know the scallop wasn't on the beach yesterday afternoon."

"Queer," muttered Spider.

It *was* strange, Diane thought. Carefully she carried the scallop back to the house. If anyone could tell her about scallops, it would be Grandfather Jordan.

8 🦞 Crabby Intruders

"It's a *live* scallop, all right," Grandfather agreed.

"But how did it get on the beach?" asked Diane.

"Someone must have dropped it. You're lucky, because it's unusual to find a live one on the beach."

Following the directions in the shell book, Diane cleaned the scallop for her collection. She put it in a pan of fresh water; then, when the scallop opened, she removed the insides with a knife, and put a drop of glycerin on the ligament which held the two shells together.

The glycerin, the instructions said, would keep the ligament from drying up, so that the two shells would stay together.

Diane put the scallop shell on the shelf with the rest of her collection. Now, more than ever, she hoped to go lobstering with Rusty before she went back to St. Louis. The lovely scallop shell was a tantalizing hint of other interesting things to be found in deeper water.

The weather was hot, and everyone in Maine felt sorry for the rest of the world. Diane's mother wrote that it was unbearable in Missouri, as it was everywhere else. Except Maine, Diane thought smugly, and she was glad Mother suggested that she stay in Whale's Creek until the heat wave was over.

One sweltering afternoon, the Ghosts arrived at the creek while Grandfather Jordan was trying to teach Diane the side stroke. "One, two, three," he counted.

The boys watched in silence. Then Darryl said, "What are you doing?"

Diane flushed. "Learning to swim," she said. The truth was out. Now they knew she couldn't swim, and they would probably laugh themselves silly.

Strangely, not one of them even smiled. "You're doing pretty well, Ditto," Bruce observed.

At low tide a few days later, Diane was digging clams for the chowder Grandfather Jordan had promised to make for supper when the three Whale's Creek Ghosts came down to the shore. Spider was holding his hands out gingerly as he carried something that wiggled frantically.

"What have you got?" Diane asked.

"Crabs!" Spider set them down in a tide pool, and they scrambled away, trying to hide.

"Crabs?"

"Funniest thing . . ." Darryl shook his head. "We found those little ones in a pile of seaweed in the tree house."

"The tree house? How in the world did they get *there?*"

"That's what we'd like to know," said Spider.

Bruce added, "We figure that someone was playing a joke."

"Or else there was a real high tide last night." Darryl grinned.

"It would take at least a tidal wave to reach the tree house in the orchard!" Diane exclaimed.

"I lean more toward the joke theory," Spider said. "Like the two ghosts in the orchard one night. You wouldn't know anything about that, would you, Ditto?"

Diane barely managed to keep a straight face. "Who —me? You boys are the only ghosts I know!"

While they talked, the boys helped her dig clams, and together they carried the heavy bucket back to the house.

Grandfather smiled when he saw the number of clams they had dug. "Too many for just the two of us," he said. "Would you boys like to join us for chowder tonight?"

Expecting all kinds of excuses, Diane was surprised when the boys quickly accepted the invitation. "Nothing we like better than homemade chowder!" Darryl exclaimed.

At supper time, Mrs. Appleton sent over a blueberry pie with the boys, and they ate outside on the patio in the warm evening. They were all in high spirits, and the boys, telling one joke after another, kept everyone laughing.

At a lull in the conversation, Diane said, "I can never remember jokes, but I do know a good way to test your balance."

"How?" Darryl asked.

"I'll need a volunteer," she said. "Who wants to be first?"

Spider jumped up. "I'll try it."

"OK." Diane restrained a giggle. Spider fancied himself quite an athlete, and he had also been the leader on that day when she'd been tricked into jumping out of the Appletons' barn window and into the pile of manure. He would be the ideal subject for the balance test.

"What do I do?" asked Spider.

"Stand in front of me," Diane told him. "I'll hold my

hands about a foot apart, and you move one of your hands up and down between mine without touching them."

"What's so hard about that?" he demanded.

Diane smiled. "You have to do it with your eyes shut."

Closing his eyes, Spider moved his hand up and down between Diane's. Then he shrugged. "Nothing to it."

"Wait a minute," she said. "Just so you won't be tempted to peek, we'll use a blindfold."

Grandfather Jordan contributed his large handkerchief, and Diane tied it around Spider's head.

While everyone else watched, Spider fumed, "I still don't see what's so hard about this."

"You will," she assured him. "The most anyone's ever done it is three hundred and three times. It's a real test of balance, and you'll be doing well if you get to fifty." Spider moved his hand rapidly up and down between hers, so she added, "You have to do it slowly— and you have to count out loud."

"One," Spider began, "two, three, four . . ."

"Slowly," she cautioned again.

"Five . . . Six . . . Seven . . ."

"You're doing fine."

"Eight . . . Nine . . . Ten . . ."

"Concentrate."

"Eleven . . . Twelve . . . Thirteen . . ."

"That's the idea," Diane said. She moved back one step, then two. Quietly she tiptoed all the way back to her chair. Standing alone on the patio, the blindfold around his head, Spider continued to move his hand slowly up and down.

"Seventeen . . . Eighteen . . . Nineteen . . ." he droned.

Doubled up, Darryl and Bruce were contorted with soundless laughter. His head in his hands, Grandfather Jordan's shoulders shook with merriment at the ridiculous picture Spider made.

"Twenty . . . Twenty-one . . . Twenty-two . . ."

"What on earth is going on?" Open-mouthed with astonishment, Rusty Babson stared at the group. "You people indulging in a seance—or something?"

Spider jerked off his blindfold and stared at Rusty, while the others broke into helpless laughter. "What *is* going on?" repeated Rusty.

Everyone, except Spider, kept right on laughing. Red-faced and looking very foolish, he stood on the patio with the handkerchief dangling from his hand. "It's— it's a balance test," he mumbled. Then he brightened. "Want to try it, Rusty? Here—you stand right in front of me, and . . ."

"No thanks!" Rusty held up his hands in protest.

"Oh, my!" Grandfather Jordan wiped his eyes. "Glad to see you, Rusty. How about some pie and coffee?"

"Thought you'd never get around to asking." Rusty cut himself a slice of pie. "Say," he added, knowing well that Grandfather's talents did not include baking a blueberry pie, "your cooking has improved some." Rusty added sugar to his coffee, and smiled at Diane. "Stopped by on the off-chance that you might be interested in going fishing tomorrow."

"Oh, I'd love to!" she exclaimed.

"You're going lobstering with Rusty, Ditto?" Darryl looked openly envious.

"Lucky you," muttered Bruce.

Though the still red-faced Spider didn't say a word, he eyed Diane with respect. Rusty shook his head. "What do you think, Diane? Should we let these three rascals come with us?"

Thoroughly enjoying the moment, and the anxious looks on the faces of the three Whale's Creek Ghosts, Diane hesitated. "Well," she said, "on one condition."

Darryl looked suspicious. "What's that?"

"That you call me Diane—instead of Ditto!"

"OK, Dit . . . Uh, I mean, Diane," Darryl said, and the other two boys nodded.

Rusty chuckled. "Guess I've got the whole kit and kaboodle."

"You've hit the jackpot," Grandfather agreed.

"Pick you all up at five o'clock in the morning," Rusty said. "And I don't wait for sleepyheads."

Cautiously, Diane mentioned the dredge that she and Grandfather had built. "Could I bring it along?" she asked.

"What do you want with a dredge?"

"It's to try to get some deep-water shells," she explained. "I'd like to take them back to St. Louis."

"But I'm in the lobstering business," Rusty protested. Then he relented. "I suppose we can't deprive those city people of a chance to see Maine's deep-water shells. Bring the thing along."

After everyone left, Diane, accompanied by Bugle, strolled thoughtfully to the top of the meadow. Since she'd started the shell collection, and had stopped tagging after the boys, the summer had taken a turn for the better. She was glad, too, that she'd had the courage to tell them she didn't want to be called Ditto any longer.

Looking at the sea, Diane wondered how she could ever have thought it lonely. The sea was living, moving, and always changing. The things beneath the water were fascinating, and tomorrow she would find all kinds of unusual shells on the lobstering trip with Rusty. She was so intent on her thoughts that a sudden bark from Bugle startled her completely. The beagle was racing toward the creek and growling at something on its other side.

Bugle and his rabbits, Diane thought, as she followed the dog. But—no! There was a person on the other side of the creek—a person who ran into the woods as she came closer. In the moonlight, Diane caught a flash of red hair. Red hair? The only redhead she knew was Rusty Babson, but what in the world would *he* be doing at the creek? And why would he run away? Was he playing a joke? Or could it have something to do with the rowboat he had asked her to keep secret? Diane smiled. Rusty was no doubt making a mystery out of nothing, just for the fun of it. Well, she'd go along with the gag. She wouldn't say a word. Rusty Babson was certainly a character.

9 🦂   A Sinister Shape

When Rusty picked them up at dawn, Diane expected
to see an extra twinkle in his blue eyes, or some other
sign that would betray him as the prankster at the creek.
But the lobsterman acted in his usual way, and Diane
found this puzzling. Either Rusty hadn't been the redhead at the creek, or else he was a very good actor.

After rowing them out to his boat in Whale's Neck
Harbor, Rusty produced four orange-colored life jackets. "Hop into these," he ordered. "Then we'll start."

Diane giggled at the way the boys looked in the life preservers, and Darryl retorted, "You don't look so hot yourself!"

Rusty checked to make sure the jackets were properly fastened. "Can't afford to lose any passengers," he drawled. "Be bad for my reputation."

The sun was rising as they headed for Hog Island, and in the distance Mt. Desert was majestic in the early morning mist. Other lobstermen waved as they passed, and Diane sighed with contentment. "What a way to live!" she exclaimed.

Rusty snorted. "You sound like the city girl from St. Louis that you are. Lobstering is a mighty tough way to make a living. Even if you're lucky and get good weather, the catch can be small, or the price of lobsters drops. And if you want to try some real living, then come out with me on a winter's day when the temperature's zero, the sea's rough, and there are icicles on your breath. It's quite a way to live," he said, "and it's small wonder that lobstermen stick together like glue. It's the only way we can survive."

Diane hesitated a moment before she asked, "Then why do you do it?"

Rusty chortled. "Wouldn't trade places with anyone for all the gold in Fort Knox," he confessed. "You're an independent man when you're in this business of lobstering—beholden to no one. And it's a pride and satisfaction to win out over the sea. No, that's not quite right. There's satisfaction in learning to live with the sea. Make no mistake, the sea is a thing to respect, and the sooner you learn that, the better off you are. I'll tell you something else, too—if you're ever in trouble, a lobsterman's the first to come to your aid. Just remember that."

Diane nodded, and Rusty went on in a less serious tone. "We even help those fair-weather, city sailors who persist in getting themselves into all kinds of trouble every blasted summer. Don't know the weather, don't know the waters, and sure don't know what they're doing." He shook his head. "Just last week I hauled a beauty of a ketch off a rock outside of Whale's Neck. Owner didn't know what had hit him." Chuckling, Rusty told them who owned the boat. "I guess he's a better senator than he is a sailor. Leastways, I hope so. But, on the other hand, I might have a certain amount of trouble navigating around Washington."

They all laughed at the vision of Rusty wandering around Washington in his lobsterman's boots. Rusty Babson belonged right where he was, Diane thought. It was hard to picture him anywhere else, and she knew that in spite of his hard life, he was contented and happy with what he was doing.

"Short trip today," Rusty said. "We'll hit Whale's Creek, and then we'll try out your contraption." He nodded at the dredge that the boys had helped Diane lug on board the boat.

Rusty checked the traps beside Hog Island. Then they went on to Raspberry and Frog Islands, and Rusty showed them how he handled the boat and the lobster traps singlehanded. Though the boys were anxious to help, Diane was squeamish about the flopping, unpegged lobsters, and the wiggly crabs that sometimes came up in the traps.

At Whale's Creek, Rusty hauled up an empty trap, and quickly dropped it back in disgust. "Happened again," he muttered.

"What's the matter?" asked Darryl.

"Lobsters seem to be getting scarce." Rusty motioned toward a second empty trap. "Might as well try out that dredge. There's no eating money here today."

The first haul was brought aboard, and Diane eagerly inspected the variety of things the dredge had scooped up from the floor of the ocean. "I wish *I* had a boat!" she exclaimed.

"Me, too" seconded Spider.

Diane smiled. For once the words "Me, too" were someone else's, and she liked it better that way. "A scallop!" she cried, when they hauled the dredge up again. "It's just like the one I found on the beach the other day."

"You found a scallop on the beach?" Rusty sounded interested.

"That's nothing," Bruce said. "We found some crabs in our tree house."

"In your *tree house?*" Rusty was incredulous. "I suppose a scallop could get washed ashore, but crabs in your tree house . . . Are you *sure?*"

"Sure as shooting." Darryl nodded. "We think someone was playing a joke on us."

Rusty frowned. "Odd kind of joke."

When Diane's box was filled with shells and other things they'd brought up with the dredge, Rusty said, "Time to call it a day. I have some other business to attend to." He let them off at Whale's Creek Beach, smiled at their repeated thanks, and then headed the lobster boat at full speed toward Whale's Neck.

"What I wouldn't give for a boat!" Darryl exclaimed.

Leaving the dredge high on the beach, the four walked up the path through the meadow to the apple orchard. "Let's take a look at the clubhouse," Spider suggested, "and see if anyone's left any more crabs."

When the boys turned off toward the tree house, Diane hesitated. Darryl looked back. "Hey," he called, "don't you want to come, too?"

Smiling as she passed the "Keep Out," "No Trespassing," and "No Girls Allowed" signs, Diane hurried to catch up. She was the last one up the ladder, and when she reached the tree house, she found the boys bent over, staring at a large dark patch on the floor boards.

"Damp," Spider pronounced, his hand on the patch.

"Someone or something's been here recently," Darryl said.

"How recently?" Diane asked.

"Hard to tell." Darryl shrugged. "Could have been as far back as last night. The sun never gets in here because of the trees, and it takes forever and a day for things to dry."

Diane puzzled over this for a moment. "Could an animal have slept here?"

"Doubt that." Spider shook his head.

The four stared at the dark patch. Then Darryl said, "How about staying up tonight to see who or what has been visiting our clubhouse?"

"Mom wouldn't approve of *that*," Spider told his brother.

"We've gone down the trellis before. She wouldn't even have to know about it." Darryl grinned. "Come on. Bruce can spend the night with us. We'll meet you at ten o'clock," he added to Diane. "It'll be pitch dark by then."

Though Diane wasn't convinced that it was the thing to do, she nodded. Grandfather Jordan wouldn't favor the idea of their keeping watch at night any more than the Appletons or the Eatons would.

Back at the house, she made herself a sandwich, and then curled up in the hammock that was suspended between two trees beside the patio. In five seconds she was asleep.

Grandfather Jordan let her sleep until supper time.

"You're not used to lobstermen's hours," he said as he woke her.

Diane stretched. "Now I know why fishermen go to bed with the birds!"

After dinner, Grandfather yawned. "Bedtime for this old potter," he said.

"It's only eight-thirty," Diane protested.

"We got up at the same time this morning, but *you* had a nap."

"Perhaps I'll stay up and read for a while."

"Well, don't forget to turn out the lights when you go to bed," he said cheerfully.

Alone in the kitchen, looking at a book but not really seeing it, Diane debated what to do. Grandfather was snoring, and it would be easy to leave without his knowing it. But should she? The boys were expecting her, she argued with herself; yet, if Grandfather should wake up, he would be worried to death to find her gone. Sighing, Diane eyed the clock. It was now almost nine-thirty, and she had to decide one way or the other. Hastily, she wrote a note to her grandfather and put it on the kitchen table. She wondered whether she should take Bugle with her. No, he was liable to bark and ruin everything. "You stay here," she whispered.

Silently, she opened the kitchen door and slipped outside. In the bright moonlight, she walked to the orchard. It was dark under the trees, and she began to wish that

Bugle *was* with her. Close to the tree house, Diane nervously waited for the boys, remembering that they hadn't said exactly where they would meet her. She had simply assumed that the meeting place would be the clubhouse. Could they be playing another trick? But it was still early, she assured herself; there was plenty of time for the boys to arrive.

In the dim orchard, the night sounds were magnified, and feeling more and more jumpy, Diane decided to wait for the boys at the top of the meadow. She could hear them from up there, and she could also see the Appleton farm.

She settled herself comfortably beside a rock, and then noticed that all the upstairs lights were on at the Appletons'. The boys might have been caught climbing down the trellis. Perhaps she ought to forget the whole thing, and go home. A light splash made Diane glance toward the sea. A porpoise? she wondered. When the splashes became noisier, she squinted across the water. Could someone be swimming? At night? Was it her imagination, or was there really a tiny, glowing light under the water? *Was there?* Almost hypnotized, Diane watched as a dark shape bobbed above the water and then stalked slowly out of the sea.

10 ✿ Standing Guard

Stunned, Diane watched the black figure drop something into a box at the edge of the beach, pick up the box, and then start toward the path where she was sitting. Instinctively, she held her breath, pressed hard against the rock, and closed her eyes. There was a squishing, flapping sound as the figure passed on the other side of the rock.

When Diane opened her eyes, the black shape was disappearing into the orchard. The minute her knees stopped shaking, she began to creep through the meadow grass, pausing often to listen and keeping as far from the orchard as possible. Creeping along as noiselessly as she could, she decided it would be safer to take the long way around, so it seemed hours before she reached the back of her grandfather's white house. There was no sound from the orchard—none at all.

Once inside the kitchen, Diane bolted the door. Her clothes were damp from crawling through the nighttime dew. Bugle licked her hand, and she took a deep breath. Everything was exactly as she had left it; the note was still on the kitchen table, and from the bedroom came Grandfather's rhythmic snoring. Everything was exactly the same.

It was unreal and fantastic. Who had come out of the water? What had the sinister-looking black figure been doing? And what should *she* do? What about the boys? Should she warn them that someone was in the orchard? Should she wake her grandfather? Somehow, in the cosy, familiar kitchen, the mysterious figure walking out of the sea seemed too far away to be real. There must be a logical explanation for what she had seen. There had to be, Diane told herself. Perhaps it had something to do with Rusty's joke. Nothing extraordinary ever happened in Whale's Creek, and it would just be ridiculous to wake up her grandfather.

She put out the lights, checked the locked doors, and went upstairs. From her window, she could see lights

still on upstairs at the Appleton farm. Well, she guessed she needn't worry about the boys coming out. Still trying to erase the nagging doubt that something was very wrong, she put on her pajamas and tumbled into bed.

"Diane! Wake up, sleepyhead!" Grandfather Jordan was shaking her gently. Sunlight filled the room, and Diane struggled to open her eyes.

Grandfather smiled at her. "You must have stayed up too late reading last night, my dear. It's time for me to get down to the pottery. I've left some eggs and bacon for you on the stove."

Drowsily, Diane mumbled, "Thanks," before she rolled over and snuggled under the covers. Then she remembered the dark figure striding out of the water. Leaping out of bed, she scrambled into dungarees, splashed water on her face, and gave her teeth a speedy once-over with her toothbrush. She was downstairs eating the eggs right from the pan when there were footsteps on the back walk. Nervously, she peered out of the window.

"Oh!" she exclaimed with relief. "It's *you* three."

"Who'd you expect?" Darryl grinned. "A ghost? Come on out."

Diane sat down on the back steps, nibbling at a piece of bacon she'd brought out with her. "Expect one, get three . . ."

"Sorry we couldn't make it last night," apologized Spider.

"We fell asleep waiting for Mr. and Mrs. Appleton to fall asleep," Bruce explained.

"Too bad," Diane said. "I thought maybe you'd been caught going down the trellis."

"Never had a chance to try even. Did you get out?" asked Darryl.

She nodded, relishing the attention.

"Well, what happened?" Spider demanded.

Diane stuffed the last piece of bacon into her mouth. "A lot." She told them from start to finish what had gone on at the shore the previous evening. Not one of the three boys said a word. Open-mouthed, they listened until she finally said, "That's the end. That's all."

"All? That's enough!" Darryl exclaimed.

"Are you sure you're not making this up?" Spider eyed Diane coldly.

She glared at him. "You don't have to believe me!"

"Don't let him get you excited," Darryl said soothingly. "He's just crabby today. Come on, let's take a look at the clubhouse."

The apple orchard didn't seem so eerie this morning, not with the boys and Bugle on hand, but even so, Diane glanced around somewhat fearfully. The first thing they all noticed was that one rung of their ladder was broken, and that there was a large and wet spot on the floor of the tree house. Some one had been here—there was no doubt about it.

"Maybe there's a clue at the beach," suggested Bruce.

The four raced to the shore, but they couldn't find anything to tell them more about the mysterious figure that had come out of the sea. The tide had washed away any evidence that might have been left on the beach.

"Describe the thing—the person—again, Ditto," commanded Darryl.

"Are you talking to *me?*"

"Uh—I mean—Diane," he amended.

"It all happened so quickly that it's hard to remember."

"Well, do the best you can."

"All right." She nodded, and told them again how the dark shape had walked out of the water, dropped something into a large box, and then carried it into the orchard.

"Do you suppose it might have been a frogman?" asked Bruce.

"That's it!" Diane cried. "That would explain the squishy, flapping noise when he went past the rock I was hiding behind. He was wearing flippers!"

"But what would a frogman be doing in Whale's Creek at night?" Spider asked.

"He wasn't playing jokes." Darryl looked grim.

While they were talking, Rusty Babson's boat appeared. They waved to him, and watched as he hauled up his traps. "Doggone!" they heard him mutter.

"Something wrong?" Bruce called out.

Rusty shrugged in disgust. "No lobsters—again."

No lobsters? They looked at one another. No lobsters —*again!* Could that be what the frogman was after? Was he stealing lobsters?

"Hey, Rusty!" Darryl yelled as the lobster boat swung away from the creek.

Rusty headed back and cut his boat's engine. "What's the trouble?"

"Can you spare a minute?"

"Is it important?"

When Darryl nodded, Rusty beached the boat and jumped down from the bow. Looking tired and impatient, he said, "What's up?"

"Has someone been stealing lobsters?" Darryl asked.

Rusty looked around at all of them. "What do you kids know about it?"

"Someone was here last night," Diane explained, and then she told him her story.

"A frogman! Well, what do you know!" Rusty exclaimed. "Guess I'll have to let you in on it, but you've got to promise not to tell one living soul, or we'll never catch the thief." His face had a grim expression. "Every lobsterman in the area has been hauling up empty traps off and on all summer, and for the last two weeks it's been worse than ever."

Wide-eyed, Diane asked, "Do you have any idea who's doing it?"

"If I did, I'd shoot him on sight." Rusty sounded as if he meant his threat. "And I'm not the only one. Lobstering, as I told you, is a tough way to make a living, and we need every lobster in our traps."

"Have you any leads?" Darryl asked.

"We've been losing sleep over worthless leads—until now," Rusty replied. "We couldn't figure out how or where the thief was getting away. But a diver! That answers a lot of questions."

Diane then remembered the night the battered rowboat had been on the beach, and Rusty's odd request for secrecy. "Were you on the other side of the creek one night when Bugle and I were walking along the beach?" she asked.

"Yes, I was standing watch in this area," Rusty admitted, "but I didn't want anyone to know what I was doing. When you kids told me about the scallop on the beach and the crabs in the tree house, I was pretty certain that the thief was using Whale's Creek as his escape route."

"Gosh!" Darryl exclaimed. "We almost forgot to tell you that someone broke the ladder up to our tree house last night, and there's another wet patch on the floor."

Rusty fastened the bow line of the lobster boat around

a rock, exclaiming, "What are we waiting for?"

At the tree house, Rusty inspected the broken rung of the ladder. "Either he was a heavy man, or he was carrying something heavy. You boys did a fair job of constructing this ladder."

"The box was about this big." Diane spread her arms to show the approximate size.

"Probably a wooden crate," Rusty speculated. "Nobody would carry lobsters around in a cardboard carton. Do you suppose he saw you last night?"

She shook her head. "If he had, I don't think he would have come out of the water. And he certainly didn't when he passed the rock where I was hiding."

After examining the wet spot, sniffing and touching it, and then putting a finger to his tongue, Rusty stood up. "Salt water, all right. I'd guess that the frogman deposited the box of lobsters in the tree house and picked them up from there later."

"With a car?" Spider asked.

"He couldn't get too far on foot with a heavy crate of lobsters," Rusty replied. "That's why he used your tree house. He probably got his car, drove down the road to the shore, and parked close to the orchard. Then he picked up the lobsters from here, stowed them in the car's trunk, and high-tailed it out of here. He wouldn't want to hang around with stolen lobsters in his possession—not in view of the way people in these parts feel about lobster thieves."

"Do you think he'll be back?" Bruce asked.

"Depends." Rusty was vague. "I imagine he's been making a very good thing out of stealing lobsters. Likely, he drives up the coast to the more-populated resort areas and sells them for a pretty penny. I doubt that he'll come back to the tree house, now that he's left the evidence of the broken ladder."

"What are you going to do?" Diane inquired.

"First, I'm going to ask you to promise not to say a word to anyone. How about it? Can I count on you?" When the four of them nodded, he explained that all the lobstermen had agreed to keep the thefts quiet, and so far as he knew, the secret hadn't leaked out.

"We haven't heard a whisper," Darryl told him.

"Good." Rusty nodded. "If I could get my hands on that rotten poacher . . ." He left the sentence unfinished. "It's hard enough to wrestle with the hundred or so things that go wrong on the sea without coming up against a thief as well. Take Archie Blaine now—six kids, and one of them a little girl with a brace on her leg. He's got doctor bills up to his ear lobes. And Ron Fisher—his boy's down at the University this year, and there's another son who wants to go to college, too." Rusty shook his head. "No sense crying over spilt milk. There are lots of others who need the money those stolen lobsters would have brought—just as much as I do. If we ever catch up with that frogman—well, things won't go easy for him."

"Have you any plans?" asked Darryl. "Could we do anything to help?"

"I appreciate the offer," said Rusty, "but you've done plenty already. The watching I intend to do for the next few nights will be better done alone."

After Rusty left, Diane and the boys discussed the situation in whispers. They realized that it was serious. Lobstermen depended upon their traps for a living, and it was hard and sometimes dangerous work.

"Those men don't cotton to lobster thieves," Darryl said.

Bruce agreed with him. "If they catch the frogman with the goods, there's likely to be trouble," he predicted.

Diane felt apprehensive all the rest of that day. She would have liked to confide in Grandfather Jordan, but the promise to Rusty mustn't be broken. She still couldn't believe that all this was going on in isolated, quiet Whale's Creek.

That night, tossing and turning in bed, Diane kept thinking about Rusty, standing guard alone on the beach. What was happening? What was going on at the shore in the dark?

11 ❧ Blackberries—
and a Discovery

The very first thing the next morning, Diane rushed to her bedroom window. The bit of blue ocean beyond the meadow sparkled; the Appleton farm, stately and tranquil, looked as it always had; and she was positive that nothing violent could have happened in the night or would happen on such a lovely day. Sunny and quiet, Whale's Creek appeared to be the most peaceful place in the world.

Just as Diane and her grandfather were finishing

breakfast, the Whale's Creek Ghosts, pails in hand, arrived at the back door.

"Mom asked us to pick blackberries for pies," Darryl announced.

"Nothing better than your mother's blackberry pies." Grandfather nodded. "The berries are just coming into season, and the best place to find them is farther up the creek beyond the bridge."

"That's what Mom said," agreed Spider.

"Want to come with us?" Bruce invited Diane.

"Sure!" The bell from the pottery tinkled as she hurried to stack the breakfast dishes in the sink. "You go ahead, Grandfather, and I'll take care of the dishes."

"Appreciate that—and I'll count on blackberries with milk and sugar for lunch. Have a good time berrying."

The second that her grandfather was out of earshot, Diane said, "What happened last night?"

Darryl shook his head. "So far as we know—nothing."

"And we stayed awake most of the night," said Bruce.

"No sign of Rusty at the beach this morning, either," Spider added. "Rusty—or anyone else."

"Do you think the frogman's gone for good?" she asked.

"I hope not!" exclaimed Darryl. "Hate to think of his stealing all those lobsters and then getting away scot-free."

Diane washed the last dish and set it on the drain

board to dry. "Maybe he's using a different escape route."

"Maybe he's quit altogether," Bruce offered.

Wondering if the frogman would ever be caught, they set off for the creek. When they found the blackberries, Diane, who ate more of the delicious berries than she put in the pail, wandered from bush to bush, picking off the biggest and blackest of the crop. She parted a clump of bushes by the creek, and stopped dead-still in surprise. There, pulled up on the bank, was a small rowboat that someone had apparently hidden among the bushes. And it looked, she thought as she went down the bank a little way to see it better, just like the dilapidated dory that had been on the beach.

She started to call out to the boys, but then clapped her hand over her mouth. What if someone *else* was still around? She scrambled back up the bank with Bugle, found the three boys, and led them back to the scarred and peeling little boat.

"Hey!" Darryl exclaimed. "I wouldn't mind having a boat like this."

"We could fix her up in no time," said Spider.

Diane said impatiently, "That isn't why I wanted you to see the boat. It looks just like the one that was on the beach a few weeks ago—the one Rusty asked me not to mention."

"Are you sure?" Spider asked. "It was dark when you saw the boat on the beach."

Spider always seemed to doubt everything she said, and Diane was annoyed. "Well, I wouldn't stake my *life* on it!" she snapped.

"Let's not stand around arguing," said Darryl. "If there's even a chance that it's the same boat, Rusty ought to know about it."

Bruce lowered his voice. "Maybe it belongs to the frogman."

"And maybe he's still around," Diane whispered.

With Darryl in the lead, they hurried back to the road, debating about the fastest way to get in touch with Rusty.

"Can't use the telephone," said Spider. "Everybody and his brother would know about that boat."

"No secrets on a party line," Darryl agreed. "We'll just have to walk to Whale's Neck and find Rusty."

They left their pails of blackberries under the elm tree beside the Appletons' house, and had walked only a short distance when Sheldon Clyde came along in his milk truck. "Give you a lift?" he inquired.

"Thanks," they replied in unison.

Diane picked Bugle up in her arms, and they all squeezed into the truck. Noisily, Mr. Clyde shifted gears. "Take a while to get to town," he said. "Got a few more stops to make."

A *few* stops? Diane thought. Sheldon Clyde delivered milk to every house along the road, and he was never in any hurry about it.

"It's better than walking," Darryl muttered.

Above the noisy motor of the truck, Mr. Clyde shouted, "What business do you have in the village?"

"Errands for Mom," Darryl called back, rolling his eyes at the other three.

Sheldon Clyde was the last person in the world anyone would tell a secret to; at each stop on his route, he passed on and picked up every scrap of news. Diane stifled a giggle. Grandfather Jordan often said that Mr. Clyde was better and more accurate than any daily newspaper.

When the milkman dropped them off by the church in Whale's Neck, they raced to the wharf, Bugle running right along with them. Rusty's boat was moored in the harbor, but the lobsterman wasn't in sight. Checking around, they found he had been at the Fishermen's Cooperative—and gone. He had been at the general store —and gone. Everywhere they stopped, it seemed they had *just missed* Rusty.

"What if we don't find him at all?" Darryl sounded very worried.

Through the window of The Whaler restaurant, Diane caught a glimpse of red hair. "There he is!" she cried.

The four crowded around Rusty at the lunch counter. "We've got to see you," Darryl said. "Can you come outside?"

Rusty set down his coffee cup, and gave the begging

Bugle the piece of doughnut that was left on the plate. "Can't even have a cup of coffee in peace," he said with a grin.

Outside The Whaler, everyone jabbered at once. "Blackberrying . . ." "Rowboat . . ." "Looks like the . . ." " . . . frogman?"

"Hold it!" Rusty winced. "One at a time. Diane, you first."

"Well," she began, "this morning we were blackberrying along the creek, up beyond the bridge, and . . ."

"Hurry up," Spider prodded her.

Rusty frowned. "Let her tell it her own way."

Though Spider subsided, he groaned. Diane went on to tell exactly what had happened, and how she thought the rowboat might possibly be the same one she had seen at the shore a few weeks ago.

"Interesting." Rusty pursed his lips. "Sounds like we're getting warm."

"What do we do now?" Bruce wanted to know.

"First, I'm going to recommend you to the Sheriff's office. They could use your kind of help." Rusty grinned again. "Then, I'm going to drive you home."

On the way back to Whale's Creek in the lobsterman's car, Rusty told them his plans. "The owner of the rowboat may still be around, and it would be best to steer clear of the creek. Since it's going to be a long night of standing watch, I intend to get some sleep this afternoon."

"Could we help you watch tonight?" Darryl asked.

"Think not." Rusty shook his head. "Archie Blaine is the only other person who knows about the possibility of the frogman, and he'll be more than willing to stand guard with me. He's as anxious as I am to catch that lobster thief."

"Couldn't we do something?" pleaded Spider.

"You've already done more than your share," Rusty said, "and it might be dangerous. We don't know how many people might be involved in this." At their crestfallen faces, he added, "There is one thing you could do—if it wouldn't be too much trouble."

"What's that?" Diane asked eagerly.

"If the odds turn out to be against us, and we need help, I'm wondering how we might alert you."

"How about using our whistle? The Whale's Creek Ghosts' special whistle." Darryl gave a shrill demonstration of the club signal.

"Guess I could manage that." Rusty tried the whistle. "Only one problem—I don't happen to be a member of your exclusive club."

"That's all right," Diane told him. "Neither am I."

Darryl grinned. "You're both honorary members—until we catch the frogman."

"How about that?" Rusty shook his head. "A neat solution to that problem. But you're a little more optimistic than I am about that frogman. He's been smarter than we've been for a good many weeks."

"What do you want us to do if we hear the whistle?" asked Bruce.

"Call the Sheriff immediately. I'll fill him in, and since he's a one-man police force, I'll convince him that Archie and I can handle this without him. But I will tell him that you may be getting in touch with him." Rusty pulled into the Appletons' driveway, and the young people scrambled out of the car. "Might be advisable for all of you to get some shuteye this afternoon," he added.

After Rusty had gone, the four stood talking in the driveway, scheming how to keep awake all night. "You three can spell one another," Diane said.

"You mean those two can spell each other," Bruce corrected her. "Mom put her foot down about my spending so many nights at the Appletons'. Says we'll have to pay board if I keep it up."

"Leave your radio on all night," Spider suggested.

"I'm going to take Rusty's advice and get some sleep right now," Diane said. "See you later." She picked up her pail of blackberries from under the elm tree, and with Bugle trotting beside her, started toward the pottery.

Grandfather Jordan was waiting at the door. "Almost gave up on blackberries for lunch," he said with a smile.

"Five minutes, and I'll have them washed and ready," Diane promised.

At lunch she couldn't concentrate on either Grandfather's conversation or the delicious blackberries. Later, stretched out in the swinging hammock, she had trouble falling asleep. With so much to think about, a nap was impossible.

That night, however, the story was different. Now she had to fight to stay *awake*. Sitting by the open window, with Bugle and the radio beside her, she struggled to keep her eyes and ears open, to stay alert for Rusty's whistle. But no sound came from the dark, lonely night; nothing except the wind whining through the fir trees.

For nearly all of the next day, Diane dozed in the hammock beside the patio. She got up only to make sandwiches for lunch, and to chat with the boys when they brought the mail up from the roadside box.

"Letter from St. Louis." Darryl tossed it to her.

Sleepily, Diane dangled her legs over the side of the hammock. "Did any of you hear anything last night?"

"Not one blessed thing." Darryl yawned.

"I'm sure Rusty would have let us know if anything did happen," said Bruce.

Spider groaned. "I wish something *would* happen. Don't know as I can go through another sleepless night."

Darryl snorted, and gave him a poke. *"Who* didn't sleep last night?"

"Don't pick on your baby brother." Deftly, Spider sidestepped another punch. "Remember—I need my beauty sleep."

"Me, too." Diane curled back up in the hammock.

"Well, lucky Sleeping Beauty!" Darryl laughed. "We

have to snooze on the beach. Mom would get suspicious if we went back to bed."

"Sweet dreams," Diane said, closing her eyes. She heard the boys tramp down the path to the meadow, and then remembered the letter from St. Louis. Lazily, she opened the envelope and took out the letter.

"Diane darling," the letter began. "We hope to have a surprise for you—and very soon. Though Grandfather Jordan is a perfect dear, the summer must have been long and dull for you. I know you're anxious to come home, and we can't wait to have you back. I won't say more now, but if things work out, you'll have your surprise quite soon."

Diane smiled. Of course, she wanted to go home! But a long and dull summer? Whale's Creek had turned out to be the most exciting place she'd ever been, and she didn't really want to go back to St. Louis right away. At least not until they captured the frogman—if he was still around. There was a good chance that he had given up. And the rowboat hidden by the creek might not be the same one that she'd seen on the beach the stormy night she and Grandfather had had supper with the Appletons. It might not even belong to the frogman at all!

12 ❦ Four Whale's Creek Ghosts

The Maine fog rolled in. It came quickly—and it stayed, wrapping Whale's Creek in misty white silence.

"No one would be out on the water unless it was an absolute necessity," Rusty declared. "Not even the frogman. We'll all get some sleep for a change."

Diane helped Grandfather Jordan in the pottery, and she took walks along the beach, looking for shells and listening to the gulls shriek through the fog. Even shrouded in fog, Whale's Creek had an enchanting and solemn beauty.

On the third night of the fog, Diane went to bed early and fell asleep almost at once. It seemed as if she'd been dreaming for only a minute, when something woke her. She saw Bugle, his paws on the sill, looking out of the low, gabled window. Diane flew out of bed, shivering in the dampness, and crouched down beside the dog. Outside, there was nothing to see except the fog scudding through the firs. Then she heard it—the special whistle of the Whale's Creek Ghosts! Twice the sound of the whistle floated to the window. Bugle quivered, and Diane listened intently. Could it be Rusty? Despite the fog, was he watching by the creek? He must be, and he must need help.

She wasted no more time, but rushed downstairs to the kitchen, fumbled in the dark for the telephone, and rang the operator. Her heart pounding, she said in a low voice, "Please, get me the Sheriff."

"Higgins here," a sleepy voice answered.

"This is Diane Jordan out at Whale's Creek. I think Rusty needs help."

At once the Sheriff's tone changed. "Be right out," he said crisply.

Diane hung up. Hoping that she hadn't raised a false alarm, she woke Grandfather, and had barely started her complicated explanation when lights flashed, brakes squealed, and a car hurtled down the road to the shore.

Grandfather Jordan threw a raincoat over his night-shirt. "Not altogether sure what we might be missing," he said, "but I don't intend to miss a minute of it."

They both grabbed flashlights from the kitchen shelf, and hurried through the meadow path, Bugle following. In a minute, they saw lights go on at the Appleton farm. When they reached the top of the banking, Bugle growled, and Diane gasped. Below, on the beach, weirdly outlined against the shifting fog and the headlights of the Sheriff's car, Rusty was holding one hand pressed to his chest, lobsters from an overturned crate were crawling over the sand, and Sheriff Higgins was tucking a gun away in his holster. In a dripping wet suit, the frogman stood with his wrists handcuffed, behind his back.

"Are—are you all right, Rusty?" Diane asked weakly.

"Caught the thief red-handed," said the Sheriff.

Behind them, Mr. and Mrs. Appleton, with Spider and Darryl, were rushing through the meadow to join them.

"What's happened?" Mr. Appleton looked bewildered. "What on earth's going on?"

Sheriff Higgins shook his head. "Going to leave the explanations to you, Rusty, and take this fellow back to town." He nodded at the morose-looking frogman.

"Need any help?" Rusty asked.

"Thanks, but I can manage."

"Sure am glad you came so quickly."

"Any time." The Sheriff motioned to the frogman to

get into the car, and the group on the beach watched as the two drove off up the bumpy woods road.

Diane breathed a sigh of relief. Then she noticed that Rusty's hand was bleeding. "You've been hurt!"

"For heaven sakes!" Mrs. Appleton exclaimed.

"Just a scratch." Rusty shrugged off the wound, and then said with satisfaction, "Inflicted a bit of damage myself."

"We must get up to the house and take care of that hand," Mrs. Appleton insisted.

"Not until these lobsters are collected," Rusty said firmly.

The boys helped him put the lobsters back in the crate, and they carried it to the Appleton farm. While cocoa heated on the stove, Mrs. Appleton tended to the slash on Rusty's hand. "This is much more than a scratch," she told him.

Rusty winced at the antiseptic. "I guess the frogman had a knife."

"I would say," Grandfather Jordan suggested, "that it's high time somebody told us old folks what's been going on around here."

As Mrs. Appleton served the cocoa and blackberry pie, Rusty told the story of the lobster thefts, the empty traps that had been hauled up all summer, and the futile attempts to catch the thief. "The first break came when the kids discovered some crabs tangled in seaweed in their tree house," he said. "After that, we put two and

two together and eventually came up with the frogman. Though if it hadn't been for Diane's keen ear, things might have turned out differently tonight."

"You mean Bugle's keen ear," Diane said. "He's the one who heard you first. How did you happen to be watching tonight?"

"Figured the frogman might be thinking the same way I was—that no one in his right mind would be out in this fog."

"How did he get the lobsters away from Whale's Creek?" Grandfather Jordan asked. "And what about that rowboat? And . . ."

"We didn't question the frogman down on the beach," Rusty interrupted, "but I'll wager that the Sheriff will have all the answers by morning."

Speculation about the frogman's summer operation kept them around the Appletons' kitchen table until, at four o'clock in the morning, Grandfather Jordan mentioned that it might be sensible to get to bed.

At the door, Darryl grinned at Diane. "Boy! Bruce will cut his throat when he finds out what he's missed."

Late the next morning, when Diane and her grandfather got to the beach, they found a crowd of people milling around the decrepit little rowboat. "Entire population of Whale's Creek," Grandfather said, nodding at the Eatons and the Appletons, "plus a goodly segment of Whale's Neck." He introduced Diane to Hempstead Fuller, editor of the *Weekly Whaler,* the local newspaper.

Mr. Fuller smiled as he shook Diane's hand. "Editor, photographer, and reporter—all rolled into one. Understand you're the young lady who got in touch with Sheriff Higgins last night. Mind if I take some pictures of you and the boys for the paper? I'd like to send a copy of the story to the papers in St. Louis, too. I'm sure they'd be interested in knowing one of their local residents was instrumental in seeing justice done."

Bruce Eaton brightened up as Mr. Fuller posed them with Rusty beside the rowboat. As Darryl had predicted, Bruce had been inconsolable about missing the capture of the frogman.

"Best story of the summer," chortled Mr. Fuller, snapping several pictures.

An official car bounced over the woods road, and when it stopped, Sheriff Higgins jumped out. "Been looking for you, Rusty. Thought you might be anxious to know how things are shaping up."

"We all are." Rusty grinned at Diane and the boys.

"Your frogman friend is being detained in Ellsworth, and he's scheduled to appear in District Court."

"Did he talk?" asked Darryl. "Did he give you all the details about how he stole the lobsters?"

"And how he got away?" added Spider.

"And where he sold them?" Bruce put in.

Everyone on the beach listened as the Sheriff answered the questions. "He talked, all right. Must have found my company less threatening than Rusty's."

"You would have been just as wild if those stolen lobsters had belonged to *you*," countered Rusty.

Sheriff Higgins grinned. "Guess a good many lobstermen felt that way. Anyway, that crook walked off with a sizable number of lobsters before you caught up with him."

"How did he manage to do it all summer?" asked Diane.

"Kept changing his place of business," explained the Sheriff. "That is, until he stumbled onto the boys' tree house in the orchard. And that turned out to be such a convenient place to stow the lobsters that he planned to use it once more last night. So he was poaching in this area."

"Didn't he think someone would be suspicious about the broken ladder?" asked Rusty.

"Sure he did, but remember, I said he *planned* to use it *once more*. He figured there was no chance anyone would be out on such a foggy night. But Rusty out-foxed him there. Before he found the tree house, the frogman sometimes put the lobsters into that wreck of a rowboat, paddled up the creek as far as the bridge, and then got his car and came along and picked them up."

"Car?" Grandfather Jordan sounded surprised. "Seems as if someone might have detected a car parked by the bridge."

"Just what the frogman feared." The Sheriff nodded. "That's why, when he discovered the tree house, he favored it for hiding the stolen lobsters. He stashed them there, went through the woods to the abandoned stone quarry where he'd left his car, and then drove back late at night to get his loot."

"But we've never seen nor heard a car near the orchard at night," protested Mrs. Appleton.

"That frogman was pretty cagey. He always drove with his lights off, and he picked his time carefully. Most of us around here go to bed with the chickens. He didn't."

"What about the tiny light I saw on the water?" Diane asked. "Did that have something to do with the frogman?"

"He had an underwater light attached to his mask, so he could see what he was stealing." Sheriff Higgins grimaced. "He thought of everything—or pretty near everything. He took those stolen lobsters farther up the coast to the crowded resort areas, and turned a pretty profit on the transaction." He added, "You kids deserve a good share of the praise for putting a stop to the thefts."

"I second *that*," Rusty said.

Darryl scuffed his feet in the sand. "What about the

boat?" he muttered. "Did the frogman steal that, too?"

"Guess you could call it a stray." The Sheriff glanced at the old rowboat. "Doesn't seem to belong to anybody, and I can't think of many who'd even want it. The frogman found it washed up on the shore at the beginning of the summer."

Rusty spoke up. "How about letting the kids have the boat?"

"Don't see what's to prevent it," said the Sheriff. "Seems fitting that they should have it."

Darryl let out a yell. "Come on! Let's try her out for just a couple of minutes; then we'll bring her out of the water and fix her up properly."

"Won't recognize her when we get through!" Spider whooped. "Bit of scrubbing, some caulking . . ."

"Coat of paint, and she'll look like new," added Bruce.

"Won't take long," gloated Darryl.

Feeling somewhat left out, Diane glanced up as the rackety milk truck swayed down the woods road. At the bottom, Sheldon Clyde stopped the truck, climbed out, and waved an envelope at Grandfather Jordan. "A telegram for you, Shaw!" he called. "Mrs. Trimble flagged me down by the telegraph office. Said she'd been trying to get you on the phone, but there was no answer. Told her you were right on my route and I'd be glad to deliver it." Mr. Clyde beamed.

"It's for you, Diane!" her grandfather exclaimed.

She tore open the envelope. It would probably be the instructions from her parents about her flight home to St. Louis. At least, Diane thought, she had stayed in Whale's Creek long enough to see the solution of the mystery of the frogman—and to help solve the mystery too! Then, as she read the telegram, her blue eyes widened. "Grandfather!" she shouted. "They're flying east in a few days! Mother and Dad! The telegram says that Mother will recuperate even faster here in Maine!"

Her mother and father were flying to Maine! Suddenly the good news really sank in, and Diane couldn't stop smiling. What a way to end the summer! There were so many things she wanted to show and tell her parents. If her mother was well enough, perhaps they could take a boat trip to Mt. Desert Island, and also explore some of the other islands in the bay. It was perfect. Or almost, she thought, watching the three boys carry the rowboat over the beach to the water.

"Now, you boys hold on," Mrs. Appleton called. "Don't think for a minute that you're going out in that boat without wearing life preservers!"

"Oh, Mom," Darryl protested, "we can swim."

"Your mother's absolutely right," asserted Mr. Appleton.

"And if you don't follow the rules, there won't be any boat to go out in," Bruce's father added.

"Please, Mom," Spider begged. "Just this once—just for a few minutes."

Mrs. Appleton finally relented, and the boys whooped with joy. Diane knew they'd have a marvelous time with the little boat—the boat they'd longed for all summer. Perhaps, once in a while, she thought wistfully, they would let her borrow it to look for deep-water shells.

The boys pushed the rowboat into the water until it floated free, and then Darryl looked around. "Well, come on, Diane," he called.

She broke into a smile and quickly ran to join them.

"Can't miss the *four* Ghosts' first voyage," Darryl said.

"Four?" She looked at the boys.

"Sure," Spider said with a laugh. "Got to have some-one along to bail."

"And row!" Bruce teased.

Diane hopped aboard, and then waved at Grandfather Jordan, who was smiling broadly. In the stern, Darryl motioned to the other boys, and the Whale's Creek Ghosts' special whistle floated over the water. In the bow, Diane laughed—and gave a small, sweet whistle in return.